AF374111

I, Wretched Man

"For my father, who taught me the art of thinking and has always been a source of strength and wisdom. Your unwavering faith in me has carried me along my path. This work is dedicated to you."

Foreword

Suffering is a universal experience, yet its meaning often eludes us. I began Ich elender Mensch during a time of deep reflection, in which I wrestled with a question that has tormented humanity for centuries: Why must we suffer? This book is not only an exploration of suffering, but a journey into the hidden power of transformation that lies within it.

Human life, when it lacks clear direction, often deteriorates into misery. History is full of accounts of people who have endured unspeakable suffering and yet, through this pain, discovered a deeper truth – transformation does not occur in the absence of suffering, but through it. At the center of this transformation stands love, the core of existence, which gives meaning to the struggles we face.

In these pages, I explore this struggle – not as distant tales, but as mirrors reflecting the human condition. I invite you to join me on a journey where we understand suffering not as an end, but as a path to transformation. This book is not meant to offer simple answers, but comfort and new perspectives for those who – like me – have wrestled with their own pain.

If you are reading these lines, I hope you discover new meaning, gain a deeper understanding of suffering, and perhaps catch a glimpse of the light that so often appears after the darkest nights.

To the weary and the broken – this is for you.

March 2025 Joyal K Chacko

Contents

Introduction: The Cry of a Wretched Soul

"Wretched man that I am! Who will deliver me from this body of death?"

Romans 7:24

I decided to write this book because certain things have deeply preoccupied me for years. They weren't concrete thoughts, but rather a dull unease gnawing inside me. Only when my life took unexpected turns did I begin to understand what was truly troubling me.

For six years, I was in the seminary, full of hope and conviction that I would one day become a Catholic priest. The first four years went well, but then came the pandemic in 2020. My seminary was in Bijnor, Uttar Pradesh. When the virus broke out, I was sent to Punalur, Kerala. The months in isolation changed me. During prayer times, I often fell asleep; my faith began to crumble. I felt a void growing within me.

Then came the quarantine – twenty days of complete solitude. For the first time in my life, I understood what true suffering meant. We, the aspirants, had believed that life was hard, but now we truly felt it. My cousin and friend Justin made a courageous decision: he left the path to priesthood. His decision made me reflect on my own future. And eventually, I did the same. I left the seminary, convinced that life would become easier. But God had other plans.

A few months later, I decided to learn German in order to pursue training in Germany. In just eight months, I reached the B2 level and got a job as a German teacher. But with this newfound freedom came new vices. I began to smoke and drink—first occasionally, then regularly. I became a passionate drinker.

In 2024, I moved to Germany, to Reutlingen, to begin training in nursing. I had some friends there from Kerala—some of them were women. But for some reason, they didn't take a liking to me. Maybe it was because of my drinking habits, maybe something else. One evening, I drank with them—nothing extraordinary, I thought. But after that, everything changed. They accused me—charges that weren't true. I was guilty of drinking with them, but innocent of what they accused me of.

And yet their voices carried more weight than mine. It didn't take long before I felt the consequences. I was dismissed from my training program; my future in Germany shattered in a moment. Everything I had worked for was gone.

I returned to India—not as a free man, but as someone cast out by his own fate.

During this time, I came to understand what it means to be a wretched man. I no longer knew suffering only through books or sermons—I lived it. My faith was shattered, my hopes buried. I became a man of sorrow and pain.

1

The Silence of God

"Truly, you are a God who hides himself, O God of Israel, the Savior."

—Isaiah 45:15

Many attributes are ascribed to God: Almighty (Luke 1:37), Allknowing (Psalm 139:4), Omnipresent (Psalm 139:7), and Unchanging (Hebrews 13:8). But one is rarely mentioned: *Deus Absconditus*—the God who hides. In this silence, in this divine absence, the human being wrestles with faith, fear, and meaning.

I have often asked myself why God chooses to remain silent precisely when we long for His presence the most. I have never found a final answer. Yet I was fortunate to receive comfort and wisdom from my parents and loved ones. Once, my father, fully aware of my drinking and smoking habits, asked me:

"Does God not know what you're doing?"

I replied, "If God exists, then without a doubt, He knows."

To that he said, "If you believe that, then God also allows your suffering."

I pondered his words for a long time and eventually came to understand: the all-knowing God sees my suffering, my pain—and yet He remains silent. Nothing happens without reason. I am reminded of Jesus' words:

"Are not two sparrows sold for a penny? Yet not one of them will fall to the ground outside your Father's care." —Matthew 10:29

These words remind me of a true story from the life of Holocaust survivor Elie Wiesel. In his book Night, he describes his time in the concentration camps of Auschwitz and Buchenwald. There, he was haunted by a tormenting question: Does God exist—and if so, why does He remain silent?

He tells of a brutal execution. Three prisoners—two men and a boy— were hanged. The men died instantly, but the boy, too light for a swift death, struggled for over half an hour. Someone in the crowd cried out in despair, "Where is God? Where is He now?"

Wiesel heard himself answer, "He is hanging here on this gallows."

These words echo Friedrich Nietzsche's famous declaration: "God is dead, and we have killed Him." Nietzsche did not necessarily mean that God doesn't exist—but rather, that He is silent—especially in moments of unimaginable suffering.

The death of an innocent child is one of the greatest tragedies. If God says or does nothing in such moments—how can we trust Him?

But what if God has not abandoned us, but sees us as His weak children? Children who wish to do good, yet often do evil?

Perhaps the greatest wisdom lies with someone who sees what we cannot—someone who knows a truth that is hidden from us.

What if God sees a greater mystery? What if the words of Jesus are true, and He never truly leaves us?

Whatever the answer may be—I hold on to the words of the Apostle Paul:

"And we know that in all things God works for the good of those who love Him." —Romans 8:28

The silence of God is not His absence. Life is hard, and eternal truth often makes it harder. But Scripture says: "You will seek Me and find Me, when you seek Me with all your heart." —Jeremiah 29:13

What does this mean? It suggests that God remains silent until we seek Him with all our heart.

Perhaps what we see as an end is not an end for God. And if it is not an end for Him, then it is not for us either.

In the Gnostic Gospel of Thomas (Saying 77), Jesus says:

"I am the light that is over all things. I am all: from Me all has come forth, and to Me all things return. Split a piece of wood, and I am there. Lift a stone, and you will find Me there."

These words point to the idea that the divine presence is hidden in all things—rooted in the light of the eternal sacrifice that points to the One who is. Silence does not mean weakness. On the contrary—it is a form of strength born from deep knowledge and wise foresight. True silence is not the absence of power, but the opposite of noise, uncertainty, and fragility—like a house built on sand, doomed to fall.

I know people who cannot endure the presence of silence. I too was once someone who struggled with it. But I must tell you—there was a time when I was getting ready for bed, alone in my room, and I felt something strange. I was filled with fear and sensed a deep inner emptiness. I felt as though I was missing something I desired most. I couldn't sleep. As I lay in bed, my thoughts spiraled: What is this thing I lack? Will I die without ever possessing it? I was deeply disturbed. And yet I found no answer.

But over time, I realized that what I longed for was love and influence. I had found an answer—but it left me dissatisfied. For I believed that the pursuit of love and influence might make me weak, and I hated being weak.

The next day I was again alone in my room—but this time, the silence was different. I could simply sit without thinking of anything. The fear from the night before had vanished. Suddenly a new thought arose: Silence itself is an art of love.

I went out for a walk—it was Sunday. Few people, few vehicles, no unnecessary noise. It was a refreshing walk. When I returned to my room, I felt twice as strong as before. And I realized: no one is truly alone. We are always connected to this mysterious universe—to enigmas that cannot be calculated, only recognized. The moment we understand that everything is connected to everything else, we free ourselves from the chains of our narrow thoughts and limitations.

The more I observe people, the more I realize that we all follow similar patterns of behavior. We share the same thoughts, only in different forms. And though we know certain truths, we are rarely willing to truly acknowledge them—those truths that lead us to the highest, eternal truths. And that is not a good direction if we truly want to rise.

The mystery of silence was gifted to humanity by the highest, eternal truth. In this silence lies meaning. God does not remain silent because He has nothing to say—but because He knows the right time to speak.

2

The Silent Sufferers

"He was a man of sorrows"

— Isaiah 53:3

There are many silent sufferers in history—perhaps more than we can even imagine. People who wished for a beautiful, peaceful, and prosperous life, but never had one. I have always been drawn to those who were men or women of sorrow. Yet some of them stand out—not just because of their suffering, but because their pain continues to guide me to this day, helping me to think, to act, and to write.

In this chapter, I will write about three people whose suffering deeply influenced me—Jesus, Nietzsche, and Viktor Frankl. All of them endured immense pain, but each of them responded to their suffering in a way that not only shaped their own destiny but also that of future generations.

I recall a quote from Augustine:

"God made his Son without sin, but never without suffering."

That is a powerful philosophical statement—it shows that God Himself allowed His Son to experience pain.

For a long time, I was convinced that "la souffrance purifie l'âme"—that suffering purifies the soul. But then I began to question: Is that really the only purpose? Does suffering exist only to sanctify us, or is there more to it—something we have yet to recognize? Perhaps it is a process with depths we have not yet explored.

One passage from Scripture fascinates me: God says, "You are like clay in the hand of the potter." If the potter is not satisfied with his creation, he destroys it and reshapes it. But before he can reshape it, he must first break it. That is a painful process.

Those who have truly tasted hardship—those who have been broken by life—search for a way to become unbreakable, so that next time, they will not shatter again. But some go even further. They were like monsters, willing to build their houses on the slopes of Vesuvius.

Jesus Christ: The Redeeming Sufferer

Many well-known figures in history lived difficult lives, but Jesus Christ stands out in a special way. What made his life so hard? Was he truly a poor man who lived selflessly and gave his life as a sacrifice for many?

When we think of Jesus' suffering, the first thing that comes to mind is his crucifixion. The Romans invented this punishment because it was especially cruel. In the Gospels, there is a passage that describes just how much Jesus suffered. It is found in Matthew 27:28–30:

"They stripped him and put a scarlet robe on him, and then twisted together a crown of thorns and set it on his head.

They put a staff in his right hand. Then they knelt in front of him and mocked him.

'Hail, king of the Jews!' they said.

They spit on him, and took the staff and struck him on the head again and again."

These words show that Jesus suffered not only physically, but was also mocked and humiliated. The apostle Paul says: He took on suffering so that we may be healed.

Can a believing Christian ever say that Jesus' suffering was meaningless? Never! Whoever claims that has not understood the faith.

The life of Jesus shows that suffering can have a deeper meaning—not just for him, but for all people. His example proves that pain and trials are part of life, but they can also lead to something greater.

Many believe that Jesus lived in poverty—that he had no permanent home and little money. But that is only partly true. The Bible gives no clear indication that Jesus was completely destitute. Rather, he lived by the principle: It is more blessed to give than to receive.

It is quite possible that he shared his possessions with the poor, because he knew that true greatness lies in giving. His voluntary suffering and death on the cross show that redemption is possible through pain and self-sacrifice.

Jesus was not only the Son of God, but also one of the greatest teachers of humanity. His life and death show that suffering is not meaningless—it can help us grow inwardly and find deeper meaning in life.

Friedrich Nietzsche: The Suffering Philosopher

I first heard of Nietzsche when I was a child, preparing for my catechism exam. That's when I stumbled upon his famous line: "God is dead. And we have killed him."

As a child who believed Jesus Christ was the eternal Son of God, I asked myself: Why would anyone say that God is dead?

Only years later, when I began to dive deeply into books, did I encounter Nietzsche again—this time not just as a thinker, but as a man. His philosophy fascinated me. But I never gave much thought to his personal life. That changed one day when I watched a YouTube video about his mental breakdown and the rejections he endured.

One moment in particular moved me deeply: his compassion for a suffering horse.

In 1889, while in Italy, Nietzsche witnessed a horse being violently beaten. He rushed toward it, threw his arms around its neck, and wept. Many see that moment as the beginning of his mental collapse.

But I wonder—was it instead the moment he became enlightened?

Nietzsche's philosophy teaches the necessity of becoming the Übermensch, of embracing one's fate—amor fati. But in that moment, he became something else: a man who saw suffering even in a silent creature. That is not a purely human capacity.

That is something divine. To recognize pain not just in oneself, but in another being who cannot even speak—that is love at its purest.

If the tears Nietzsche cried had a voice, I believe they would have said to the horse:

"I understand you. I understand your pain. I understand your silence."
But what if the horse hadn't suffered silently? What if it had rebelled,
kicked, and resisted?

Would Nietzsche still have embraced it?

I don't think so.

A rebellious horse would've embodied the will to power—asserting
itself against its oppressor.

But Nietzsche saw something deeper in the silent, suffering creature:
an acceptance of pain that transcends defiance. A dignity that defies
words.

What is the highest ideal?

Is it to love one's fate?

To become who we truly are?

Or to become the reality we are meant to be?

Perhaps all three are the same path.

To love your fate is to surrender to the process of becoming.

And in that surrender, we find what is most real.

Nietzsche wrote: "There are no facts, only interpretations."

Truth, for him, was not something fixed, but something flowing—like
a river.

If truth were rigid, it would shatter in the current.

But if truth is something that endures—like the soul or character—
then it becomes eternal.

The greatest lesson Nietzsche left us may be this: Do not resist the
laws of nature. Do not judge. Do not strike back. Do not carry

resentment. But accept the suffering that can transform you because only those who can suffer silently can set the stars dancing within.

Viktor Frankl: The Seeker of Meaning

Viktor Frankl should be regarded as one of the greatest sufferers who ever lived. When I think of such people, I wonder how they managed to endure their torment without losing their minds. In Man's Search for Meaning, Frankl describes both his personal experiences in the Nazi concentration camps and the development of logotherapy—a form of therapy that understands meaning in life—even in suffering— as the central driving force of human beings. I have read this book, and it touched me deeply. What makes Frankl's work so extraordinary is his ability to maintain an optimistic outlook even in the face of the abyss. Like Nietzsche—whose philosophy Frankl admired, particularly the quote: "What does not kill me makes me stronger"—Frankl believed that suffering can be transformed into strength if one finds meaning in it.

And yet, despite my knowledge of Frankl's insights, I have often forgotten his words in times of deepest despair. When I was expelled from Germany, I felt as though I would never see light again. My life seemed meaningless, and I—like many other desperate souls— wanted to destroy myself. But then I remembered the words of the Apostle Paul in Romans 5:3–4: "But not only that—we also glory in tribulations, knowing that tribulation produces perseverance; perseverance, character; and character, hope." Frankl's life is a living testament to this truth. He said: "Once a person discovers meaning in their suffering, the suffering ceases to be suffering." This statement reflects a profound existential reality—every human being suffers, often without understanding why. Pain is deeply rooted in existence, and no one can escape its deadly grip. Yet Frankl's idea of tragic optimism suggests that even when optimism seems unattainable, there is still something one can do: suffer silently and without bitterness.

Suffering in Silence: A Path to Redemption

When one suffers, it seems almost impossible to remain optimistic. But silent endurance—as practiced by Jesus, Nietzsche, Frankl, and many unknown souls—can be a powerful response to suffering. Frankl observed in the camps that some prisoners became truly diabolical beings, while others—like those who prayed the Shema Yisrael all day—maintained their spiritual integrity even amidst unimaginable cruelty. This silent endurance, free from bitterness, reveals a strength that transcends human limits. It is a quiet rebellion against despair, a testament to the fact that suffering, when borne with meaning and dignity, not only transforms the sufferer but also those who witness it. Perhaps in the silence of suffering, one discovers a deeper truth—that even when meaning seems lost, the human spirit can rise from the ashes and remain unbroken.

I chose to write about Nietzsche, Viktor Frankl, and Jesus because they deeply influenced me in my own suffering. They helped me stay upright and remain silent in difficult times. I think of the words of the great scholar and artist Leonardo da Vinci: "I love the person who smiles in trouble." These words show how powerful silence can be, even in the face of suffering. I have seen people who remained silent despite great pain, and I believe there is something spiritual in that. If one has deep faith—a faith that can move mountains, as Jesus said—then one can find the courage to endure severe trials. Faith not only gives strength but also hope, and it helps one bear what once seemed unbearable. The apostle Paul says in 2 Corinthians 5:7: "For we walk by faith, not by sight." These words remind us that we should not rely solely on ourselves, but on God. Through this faith, we can endure suffering and allow pain to bring forth something good within us.

3

Transformation Through Suffering

"My days are over, my plans are shattered, the desires of my heart are gone." (Job 17:11)

The Book of Job is one of the most striking books that describes the tragedy of life. Job was a wealthy man who likely lived between 2100 and 1900 B.C. After his great suffering, he lived for another 140 years and received double the blessings he had lost. His patience and trust in God not only restored his life but made it even better.

The big question is: How could Job endure so much pain without losing his faith? There are times in life when we must go through deep despair and suffering. Those who accept this pain and believe that it will lead to something good will grow inwardly. But this is easier said than done. It is hard to remain silent in suffering or to find hope in darkness. Why does God allow pain? Why does He permit us to suffer? The world is full of pain and suffering. Often we ask ourselves: What does God want to make of us?

I don't have all the answers, but I can tell you what pain has changed in my life.

Pain – The Fire That Teaches Gratitude

I used to be a person without gratitude. I lived as if life would never end—arrogant, quick-tempered, and full of bad habits. Sometimes I wanted to live a better life, but I never succeeded.

In difficult times, I was completely alone. I had no one to talk to. I lost interest in everything I once enjoyed—watching movies, learning languages, and other things that used to bring me joy. Instead, I drank and smoked a lot. After a while, I became afraid because I realized I was losing control of my life. I tried to drink less, but I could never stop completely.

In the moments when I was sober, I began to reflect on my life. I realized I had serious problems—not just with my habits, but with my whole life. Every night, as I went to sleep, I had dark thoughts. I was afraid, but somehow, I survived those days. Eventually, I began reading the Bible again—a habit I had given up after leaving seminary. But this time, it was different. As I read the Bible, I felt as though the Bible was reading me. I discovered how important gratitude is.

I learned that gratitude is not just a feeling, but a way of seeing life. No matter what happens—if you look at it with a grateful heart, it changes the pain. This perspective is a gift from God that transforms our hearts.

Pain – The Master That Helps You Become Who You Truly Are

Pain plays an important role in helping a person become who they truly are. This is clearly evident in history. As I discussed in the previous chapter—about Nietzsche, Frankl, and Jesus, who have influenced my thinking—their lives were filled with pain and suffering. Yet this pain helped them grow beyond themselves. In my case, I believe I still have much to achieve. I've always had the desire to create something meaningful. I admire great artists like Leonardo da Vinci, Raphael, and
Rembrandt, and great writers like Dostoevsky, Nietzsche, Jordan Peterson, and others. One of the reasons I'm writing this book is because I've gone through uncomfortable experiences. When the heart is filled with pain, you become invulnerable—because the pain leads you. It helps you die internally before you die physically.

Often, students try to move forward even after rejection. They do it because they endure the pain and keep going with a smile. I know a friend who was in love, but the woman suddenly left him. I thought he would destroy himself. But he didn't. Instead, he became someone who proved that he was strong and valuable despite all the pain and hardships.

Is this possible for everyone? Can everyone resist pain and become who they truly are? I don't think so. I've often sabotaged myself in difficult times because I'm restless inside. I recognized that, and I realized it's a problem. I knew I had to change—and I've changed a little. Pain can lead either to destruction or to growth. In psychology, there's the concept of post-traumatic growth. One can grow through pain, but it can also destroy you.

One thing I've learned: No one can destroy you except yourself. If we don't recognize our flaws, sin waits at the door, ready to consume us.

But we have a choice. If we're not bitter and don't hold grudges, there's always a way forward.

I know a man whose life was so difficult that he became addicted to alcohol and sees himself as worthless. His story is tragic: as a child, he was sold and abandoned by his father for 50 rupees. His parents never cared for him. He lived on the streets, fed by kind strangers, but never had the chance to go to school. He works very hard, but he numbs his pain with alcohol. He eventually got married, but after a few years, his wife left him—maybe because of his drinking and irresponsible lifestyle. He still drinks and cannot forgive his parents for destroying his life.

Once, we asked him if he could forgive his parents if he saw them on the street. He replied with rage, "I would never let them live, because they ruined my life." A predictable answer. Only when he is ready to let go of the pain—or endure it silently without becoming bitter—will his life begin to change.

Life is hard. Such situations can happen to anyone, no matter who you are. But who will save the lives of these broken people? Pain can help you—but only if you act consciously. Even in the deepest abyss, the eternal can bring blessing.

Pain – The Signpost to God

"The Lord is close to the broken-hearted and saves those who are crushed in spirit." (Psalm 34:18)

We live in a world where we're often in a hurry and forget to remain calm, even in difficult times. Pain can open many paths—one of them leads us to God. Many people in history show us how suffering brought them closer to Him. A well-known example is the story of Helen Keller. She was born on June 27 in Tuscumbia, Alabama. Her life was marked by suffering from a very young age. At just 19 months old, she became deaf and blind. As a child, she felt isolated and frustrated, living daily in pain and loneliness.

Later, Anne Sullivan, a teacher from the Perkins School for the Blind, helped her learn to read and write. I believe Helen Keller must have often felt angry or sad about her fate. It's normal to wonder why others are born with healthy senses while we must suffer. But if we remain bitter for too long, it can destroy our hearts.

Helen Keller, however, found her way to God through the teachings of
Emanuel Swedenborg, a Christian theologian. He was deeply aware of God's presence and helped Helen develop a profound faith. She held tightly to the words of Jesus:

"This happened so that the works of God might be displayed in him." (John 9:1–3)

Helen Keller came to understand that her pain had a higher purpose. She believed in that—and became a beacon of hope for millions who had lost theirs.

Another example is Leo Tolstoy. His book My Confession moved me deeply. Tolstoy was wealthy, famous, and influential—yet he was unhappy inside. He felt a great emptiness and sensed that something essential was missing. Despite all his success, he even considered ending his life, as he found no meaning in it. But the simple life of the peasants he observed each day, along with the Word of God, brought him back to life.

The words of the well-known psychologist Carl Jung fit well here: "The modern man does not see God because he does not look low enough."

The lives of these people show us that pain can lead us to something greater—perhaps even to the fulfillment of our highest potential. Pain is a teacher that may break our hearts, but also leads us to the path of eternal goodness and truth.

Pain – The Path to Compassion

The nature of the world and the universe that moves and sustains us is hard to comprehend. People who live as if they are dead, full of pain, are hard to recognize. The more I understand life, the more I see the pain. But isn't compassion, born from pain, stronger than the pain itself? It is said that in a person's eyes, one can see the abyss— the sadness, the suffering, the longing for a love that cannot be found in men or women.

But how does pain become compassion? Pain becomes compassion when one realizes that it is the highest, most transformed form of pain. Something unknown, deep, almost sacred touched me as I lived with pain like a husband with his wife. We are never alone—pain is always with us. But in our hearts, there is a door through which compassion enters the world. This compassion is more than simple empathy, stronger than anger, more destructive than jealousy, and more powerful than the will to fight.

Compassion can be seen as the ultimate essence of God, who never reveals Himself, always remains silent, and acts as though He has abandoned everything. Yet His ways are higher than we can imagine.

Modern people, living contemporarily, try to rewrite the laws of the universe with their foolishness. The absurdity that now leads the world, yet thanks to God, who allows this foolishness to persist, because the creation of wisdom can emerge through the stupidity of men.

The greatest of all is compassion, which purifies the ugly, finds the lost, cares for the broken, and loves the unlived.

I, a wretched person, because I have encountered the truth on an uncertain path but was never able to act according to the philosophy of obligation. Wretched am I... wretched are we... who will love us? Who will teach us the eternal truths? Who will look at us with the eyes of compassion?

Pain – Absolute Chaos

When something superficial happens, something that brings unimaginable pain, endless problems, isolation, and hopelessness, a door opens that reveals the true nature of people—even those we love. How painful it is to love these people who are full of snakes and lies? It is nothing that can be changed because people never change. This should be seen as the curse of existence. Pain brings a fire in the hearts of people; those who sink into pain carry a stronger flame within.

Earlier, I spoke about the good that pain can bring, and this has been proven by historical figures such as saints, who transformed the deepest pain into something good. I then thought about the unfortunate souls who experienced deep pain and completely turned against themselves, bringing destruction and chaos to the people around them and their own lives. What part of their lives had turned against them? Is it really the pain they endured? Could it be the lies they firmly hold as their beliefs? I believe it is the lies in their hearts that paved the way for total destruction. I had such thoughts too; I never thought I could be someone who would do terrible things. But the more I got to know myself, the more I recognized the monster that lies within me. It is not the pain that brings destruction; the desire to destroy and create chaos is deeply embedded in every person. Only some recognize it; others prefer to live in ignorance. Scripture warns thoroughly against the spirit of resentment. It is the master devil that sows the seeds of poison and murder. It is very hard to save oneself from the hands of resentment. I fear people who bear false witness, because everyone we see around us has something to contribute, but the question here is: Is it a lie or the truth that you want to contribute? Thoughts are more dangerous than weapons. When they do not speak the truth and are not properly understood, they bring destruction.

This is why modern people tend toward depression, mental illness, and violence. They believe in things that are not true. The nature of pain, suffering, and isolation can never create malice; it is the devil who creates malice. It is fear that creates malice. The difficulty lies in not reacting, not responding to the external stimuli that can open doors to great loss and problems. I have always been fascinated by the concept of evil. God created man with the ability to do evil things. Perhaps He found greater glory in planting a seed that can bring destruction, but He does not use this ability voluntarily.

I remember a concept my father told me. I never knew how he came to this thought, but his words have always made me think deeply. He said, "There is a punctuality in being unpunctual." – such a powerful statement. He continued—sometimes people do many things that are so cruel, so despicable, and so foolish. But do we have the right to judge them? What if God sees things in a different way, from a dimension that has not yet been revealed to the human heart?

The way animals perceive things is different, how humans see them is different, and how the Eternal sees them is also different. People who brought destruction into the world should be judged with great caution by others, because who knows if they sometimes had the right to become demonic? There are greater things that can even transform the absolute chaos that is ready to devour oneself—but only if we are willing to walk the path of light. I know nothing else that is harder than living a life with full potential.

In the last few months, however, I became aware of an emotion that made me weak and wretched, and that emotion was fear. Fear is not entirely an emotion. It is the absence of wisdom, the helplessness of existence. The value of life lies in the courage to be ready to accept the tragedies of life. Life should not be lived in comfort or pleasure, but rather to know the inevitable love of pain each day.

The Gift of Grace

Grace is something everyone needs. I believe everyone longs for it. Pain sometimes causes people to do things they shouldn't. But there is a point of fragility in every person. We do malicious things that we actually don't want to do. Do we really have free will? I don't think so. Every human life is miserable. Imagine a life where we control everything and everything depends on us. That would not be a good direction because we humans are helpless. Here lies the importance of God: God is not dead – we need Him. If He were dead, that would be the greatest curse of existence. A dead God means we are in great trouble. We would have no way to salvation. Must we really live in disappointment and hopelessness? If there is no grace, there is also no protection.

God was dead. But now He lives again. There are problems, there is suffering, there is pain – but above all, there is also grace.

There were times in my life when I experienced God's grace. Many days were very difficult. Sometimes I thought about the brevity of life and how much we have to endure in this short time. Yet, I do not see this as a curse of existence because the truth is not far from us. The truth is within us.

How can we receive God's grace? Do we receive it by living a flawless life? Perhaps, but more than that, there is something that draws us to grace. In the parable that Jesus tells, He reminds us of the prayer of the sinner – now known as the Jesus Prayer – "Jesus, Son of God, have mercy on me." Jesus praises the sinner who prayed this prayer because I believe there is great wisdom in this prayer.

God's grace comes to us when we are humble enough to acknowledge our own weaknesses and inadequacies. Humility brings grace, even in difficult times. But it does not mean that I am powerless or that I must diminish myself when speaking with others.

No, that is not the truth. True humility arises from the heart and is directed toward the Eternal – it can even occur in silence. God loves the one who believes in His power and trusts Him. The world is based on lies – people speak lies everywhere, believe in lies, and are led by lies. The truth lies in recognizing how foolish, vulnerable, and miserable we are! Who can save us? – God? A life founded on truth makes existence valuable, meaningful, and beautiful. The most eternal thing of all is the truth – and it is the same as God and love. Now I know that true greatness lies in humility and truth, but I cannot live by it.

The Longing for Pain

There are certain truths that we already know; through research, through observation, we have gained much knowledge and recognized many facts. Among these is the truth that we long for success, love, and power. History is an example of this. Everywhere, people seek happiness. If we ask people how they want to live their lives, they will say they want a happy life. But what is a happy life, really? Is happiness more valuable than life and truth? I believe the reason people say they want to be happy is not that they always want happy experiences in their lives, but rather they have become accustomed to the fact that the purpose of life is happiness. This is partly true, but not entirely true.

The purpose of our lives and the adventure we struggle with is not just to find happiness but to make our hearts strong enough to fight with our own deep self. This fight can be difficult and painful, and it involves much suffering. People do not always want only hedonistic pleasure; they also need silence, solitude, pain, adventure, and suffering.

There are people who are extroverted, introverted, and perhaps ambivalent—regardless, everyone longs for pain and challenging things in their lives. Many deny this fact because they are not aware of their inner selves, which longs for discomfort and pain. Part of the reason our inner self longs for this is the strength that our soul desires. Strength comes through pain, power comes through pain, and transformation happens through suffering. We must recognize ourselves. We must become what our inner self demands of us. All philosophers, all thinkers speak of the importance of self-realization or self-transformation, becoming something higher, something more valuable and sacred. The chariot that takes us to the highest is called pain. Pain is a helper, and acceptance is the way. Everyone lives with pain, perhaps even with unbearable pain. What honor can we give to the suffering? What kindness do the afflicted expect? What kindness can our eternal God bring us? How deep is the abyss? How miserable are we—the ones who suffer?

4

Love as the Core of Existence

When I think about love, many things come to mind. I am fascinated by love because I have always tried to understand what love truly is, but I feel that there is still more to explore about it. Love is not just a feeling—it is the truth, perhaps the greatest of all truths. Everything comes from love, and everything leads back to love. Love is infinite; it never ends. It does no harm to anyone. It is pure, sacred. The more I thought about love, the more curious I became, because the love within me has not yet been fully lived. I long for love, and I want to be loved—just like everyone else.

The question I ask myself is: why is love so important in human life? Why is mankind so interested in love? Why do I feel that love is the foundation of all truths?

I have decided to uncover the truth behind love. And love is not just a concept—it is a person. And that person can be me—or you.

God is Love

Holy Scripture says that God is love. But what does that mean?

It means that God is at work wherever true love exists. That's a profound thought—because it tells us plainly that God, in His highest form, reveals Himself through love. Life can sometimes be hard and sorrowful. Many people ask themselves: What is the meaning of life?

Why are we in this world? Some live as if they'll never die. Others already feel dead inside. But God wants us to truly live.

There are many reasons to give up—but one powerful reason to keep going:

The deepest meaning of our life is to learn how to love. We are called to become love itself and let love grow within us. We sense that the greatest truth is waiting for us.

And that is our adventure: to become love and to overcome everything with the invincible power of love.

The Bible does not say directly that our life's goal is to learn to love. But it shows us—through everything Jesus did, in His life, His death, and His resurrection—that love is the most important thing in life.

The well-known psychologist Erich Fromm writes in his book The Art of Loving that love does not just happen. We must learn it and practice it. That's not easy—but it's possible.

We don't need power or influence for this—only the desire to find love.

And when we search long enough for something, it will eventually come to meet us.

Now consider this question: Is there anything that can change the wretched self of an unhappy person?

If yes, what? Does psychotherapy always help?

One possible answer is: There are many things that might help—but they may not change a person's entire perspective. They cannot destroy the lies that linger in their life.

So what is the truth here? Why are people so unhappy? Why is our very existence so full of suffering?

These are questions without clear answers. But the deeper we dive into the truth, the more we discover the light that never fades.

The truth is this: Love remains—even in the deepest darkness. It waits for us in all its glory.

Love can transform a person's life—but it must be a love that endures.

True love is always linked to pain, because if love is real, it does not demand to be returned.

It suffers silently, without complaint. This love is full of hope. It already feels rewarded—even if it receives nothing in return. Unrequited love is painful—sometimes unbearably so.

But if we endure the pain without bitterness and even choose to forgive, then the eternal God sees His own nature in us.

Love is Neutral, and It Remains Neutral

One of the things we don't understand is the neutrality of love. For everyone, love is an emotion that brings out the best in us. But love is not just that. It is also something that can turn everything into hatred, bitterness, and pain. Love is the most dangerous thing that exists in this world. To love is to suffer; to love again is to suffer again.

People seek love in the wrong places—and then seek again in the wrong places. It is obvious that the world can give you everything except love. Love does not exist in the world. It once existed, but monsters killed it. Now, love remains only in those who have become love themselves. This world is a hell—perhaps the greatest of all hells—because it has no love. The greatest tragedy a person can experience has already happened: the inevitable tragedy—the lack of love. Existence is a curse, but love is the cure. Where is that love that can turn even the strongest poison into a tonic? Love is neutral and remains neutral. It is hidden because we do not know what love truly is. Love has not yet been fulfilled within us. I have had friends who pretended to possess love, but they were the ones who lacked it the most. How wretched I am! How wretched is life on this earth!

To live with love means to live without resentment—without resentment toward life, without resentment toward ourselves. When we are confronted with reality, reality itself can be a driving force for love—but most people never truly face reality. Love remains neutral until we recognize reality—the reality that there was a man who knew the truth about love. Jesus is the man who became love. The real problem is believing in the people we love. Even Jesus encountered many people, but he didn't heal everyone. He was despised and rejected, not because he lacked love, but because the people he loved had no love within them. His tragedy was not his death, but the undeserved pain and rejection he faced. People in love often try to possess the one they supposedly love. This kind of self-proclaimed love is the dumbest form of love—in fact, it isn't even love. It is a distorted form of love—one that neither brings good nor does good.

So how should we love? Whom should we love? Everyone? Whoever tries to love everyone loses themselves in hopelessness. Love does not show itself in words, but in actions. The great leader I admire was not a romantic lover. He did not seek love in the worst hearts of women but knew that the hearts of men and women can be more terrifying than Satan himself. Love must be neutral. You should love the one who thirsts for love. Not everyone thirsts for love. Some are full of arrogance, some full of hate. Some are the source of ultimate evil. Ignoring them is the most powerful revenge one can take.

The great teacher I admire was a man of love. He brought a revolution of love, but at the same time, he knew that love needs a second act: a call for love, a desire for love. If you want to be loved, you must make yourself lovable. And it is through humility that one becomes lovable. The greatest enemy we can face is ourselves. Our pride in our hearts is our own enemy. Let me make a new declaration: Everything we believe about love is completely wrong. We understand it horribly wrong. Love is not what we think. We believe that love dwells within us and that we need people to express our love. Here's the question: What if the love that dwells within us is not actually love, but just a vague idea of it?

I loved a woman and thought I truly loved her. But my love for her made me weak. Can love make us weak? No, never. Love is the strongest of all. Love cannot be weak, cannot be weakened or powerless. It gives us strength, makes us strong, stronger, and strongest. This is the truth: This love does not exist in men nor in women. And even if it is found in men, it can never be found in women in their twenties. Through wisdom, one encounters the eternal image of love. It can be strange, terrifying, and powerful. People constantly make mistakes. Everyone makes mistakes, but we are so blind that we don't even recognize a single truth in a day— and no one admits it. People have prejudices that are not true. They say things that are pure nonsense. They act as if their own stupidity guides them.

And I fear these convictions of the modern world. Some give advice because they believe they know everything about the person they're talking to. People judge because they're too narrow-minded to think differently. They cling to their beliefs as if they were absolute truths. But ask yourself: Are these really your convictions, or just the lies in your heart? Will these beliefs lead you to God? Will they really help you or society? No one seems to care. There are two evils that cause the worst suffering in humanity: lies and arrogance. Lies on the tongue and arrogance in the heart bring total chaos. I remember a quote from the French philosopher Jean-Paul Sartre: *"L'enfer, c'est les autres"*— "Hell is other people."

There is some truth in it, but I would put it differently: *"L'enfer, ce ne sont pas les autres, mais les gens arrogants."* "Hell is not other people, but arrogant people." If we believe that all people are hell, then that would be the greatest damnation. Living with people is not a misfortune. But we must admit that people can act like hell—even in ways that would surprise Lucifer himself.

The truth is: If you plant the seeds of arrogance in your heart and live without mercy, love, and compassion, then you have already declared yourself the devil of your own downfall. What we need are the seeds of compassion. And true compassion is often silent—without prejudice, without judgment.

The Danger of Arrogance

Human beings are arrogant by nature. We are all slaves to arrogance and follow it as if it were our leader. Arrogance comes from the heart, but we do not notice it. The philosophy of the wretched souls has been forgotten today—no one sees how wretched we are or how miserable the life is that we are struggling with.

Arrogance leads to destruction. It is the root of all sins—it condemns others, harms them, and shows us a false version of ourselves. It makes us narcissistic and calculating. I remember how my father often told me that I was arrogant. He also said that many problems in my life stemmed from my arrogance. And he was right. I, a wretched man, was also an arrogant man—and I wanted to change. But how? Who could help me? Who would criticize me with truth and love? I found no one.

Many people believe: If you don't have something, if you are addicted, if you haven't found love yet, then the problem lies with you. But that's nonsense. A wise person does not judge so easily. Not all suffering is self-inflicted, just as not every success is deserved. Some receive chaos; others receive wealth and order. So what should we boast about?

The ancient philosophers said: "Know thyself." But we, the modern philosophers, must go further—we must not only know ourselves, but also recognize the misery of human existence. Only through this understanding does true wisdom arise. If we cannot see how pitiful being human is, how can we overcome the arrogance that threatens to devour us? Whoever recognizes our wretchedness moves toward salvation.

The strength lies in recognizing how wretched we are.

The wisdom lies in accepting how wretched we are.

The grace lies in confessing how wretched we are.

We, the wretched ones—we are the light that modern society ignores.

Love Does Not Judge

The wisdom of modern philosophers lies in saying or doing what is right. But some illusions obscure reality. It is hard to see people with love, and good people do not exist. Many philosophers have made false claims—words that can deceive us if we do not recognize the truth within them.

What is good? Everything that comes from love. Love is stronger than evil, for love does not judge—not even those who tried to deceive us with their so-called wisdom. I remember Nietzsche's criticism of Christianity. He said it was a religion of pity, for the weak. Even its master, he claimed, was weak. But we can only judge rightly once we recognize the truth. And the truth is: Christianity is not just a religion, but a way of life. It means following a man who was once cursed. What is more important—the man or the religion? Of course, the man. Religion exists for people, not the other way around. Great thinkers and influential people often lack love. They see only the darkness in everything. But the wise should judge no one—not even the cruelest. The hunger for power, fame, and sex rules people today. But what is missing? Love.

Jesus judged no one. To the Pharisees he said: "Woe" — *"οὐαί"* — a word full of sorrow, not condemnation. He knew the truth does not change, except when true repentance is found within us. True strength means to forgive and to live without resentment.

Yes, the Bible can be overwhelming. Many times, I wanted to reject its teachings. But something still draws me to Christianity. What is it? The morality of Scripture? The miracles it tells?

No. I tell you, no!

It is a person—a 33-year-old Nazarene. *Yahshua.* His pure love leads me. He does not judge me for my failures. And he never will. Why? Because I see myself as wretched. A lost, wretched soul.

The Will to Power – A Means, Not the Goal

The will to power—a Nietzschean concept defining the fundamental driving force of life. Every great mind in history speaks of the urge to become something, to overcome something—to free oneself from the mere weakness of human nature and approach a supernatural strength.
Nietzsche called it the will to power, the necessity of becoming the Übermensch. And I believe this: Man is something that must become. He must shed the herd mentality and explore the uncharted realms of reality.

I have often asked myself—is power the only force that has driven humanity since the dawn of time? Power makes the wretched arrogant. But if the wretched man becomes aware of his own wretchedness, he will seek power differently—it will not lead to tyranny. Power is the path, but it is not the destination. In the end, we

are not judged by our power. The revaluation of all values may produce many
Übermenschen—but not a single true human being! There is a greater truth beyond power, even beyond meaning. And through this truth, we are redeemed.

I am not against power. I am not against meaning.

But what if power alone does not lead to the Highest?

What if meaning does not lead to the Highest?

What if we are overlooking something even greater?

We need the summit of truth—the highest point in the triangle of existence.

The problem of the modern world is that there are too many paths, too many interpretations, too many deceptions.

What is the right path? Which one leads us to the Highest?

It is easy to fall into traps—traps that, at first, seem like absolute truths. Every new value brings a new interpretation, and new interpretations bring new problems, which can sometimes lead to chaos and destruction.

Power alone is not enough. It never reaches the end. In fact, gaining power is not transformation—it is merely change.

The truth is simple; everyone knows it.

But the problem is: Man is not content with the truth he already knows.

I do not understand why we ignore reality when it offers itself freely to us, and instead chase after new, destructive theories.

Existence was not a curse. But now it is.

We have made everything worse.

We ignore the Highest Good.

All philosophers had a gentle touch of madness.

To be a philosopher means to create something new.

But modern philosophers should not be creators of new values—they should be discoverers of undiscovered truths.

We do not continue living because power exists.

We continue living because love exists.

No matter how powerful or influential we become—within our wretched souls remains a deep, empty space in which we long for unconditional love.

The desire to assert oneself, the struggle for survival—that may be understood as will to power.

But there is not just one path. There are too many paths.

Nietzsche was not wrong. He formed his own thoughts and ideals.

But I believe in something higher: the greatest truth—the will to love.

Because love survives where men break.

False love makes you weak.

True love makes you strong—the strongest.

A person with true love shines brighter than a thousand stars.

Nietzsche felt it. His words reveal it:

"What is done out of love takes place beyond good and evil."

He searched for it—just in the wrong places.

No wonder he didn't find it.

It wasn't his fault.

He is still considered one of the greatest philosophers of all time.

But still… the tender soul of Nietzsche deserved love.

The Will to Meaning – A Burden

The will to meaning is not a fixed truth—it is a constantly shifting idea. Human beings are relentlessly searching for the meaning of life, as if it were a hidden treasure waiting to be found. Many people I know believe that discovering a sense of meaning is the highest goal in life. I once believed the same. I was a person desperately searching for meaning in my existence—until I realized that this search is often just a disguise.

And then I asked myself: Why do we even seek meaning in our existence and in our actions? Viktor Frankl once said, "Once man sees meaning in his suffering, it ceases to be suffering." But life gives us many things without asking for our permission—pain, suffering, and tragedy. These are inescapable parts of life. Whoever wishes to end suffering is, in truth, wishing for life itself to end.

The Book of Revelation says: "There shall be no more pain and no more tears." But this verse does not promise the absence of existence—it promises a new kind of existence, a life beyond suffering. Earthly life is marked by pain; the new heaven and new earth promise existence without it.

There is meaning in everything—in what we do, how we live, how we suffer. But the way people find meaning is deeply subjective. What is profoundly meaningful to me may be utterly meaningless to another.

Meaning changes. It adapts. It can deceive. And that is why the search for meaning itself becomes a burden.

So what are we to do? We are to do what we must do. In the fulfillment of duty—through sacrifice, labor, and love—we become who we are meant to be. Many say they find meaning in sacrifice, in work, or in love. But if we look closely, we see: everything we call meaningful ultimately flows from love.

And so I come to the conclusion I now hold:

Meaning sustains.

Power prevails.

But the greatest of all is love.

If love is our final goal, why are we so obsessed with the meaning of life? Love is what makes us alive. Love transcends meaning. Part of the reason people seek meaning is because they are obsessed with the idea that life must have one—and to me, that is not a strong enough argument.

In India, I often heard people say, "Love is what gives life meaning."

Perhaps that is a universal thought. Most people seem to believe it.

But to me, that thought is incomplete. To say that love gives life meaning—is not enough.

I see it differently.

I believe love is what gives life life.

If love does not manifest within us, then neither life nor breath can take root within us.

Modern humanity has made astonishing progress—in knowledge, in science, in technology, in uncovering the mechanisms of the universe. And yet we have barely touched the most mysterious of all forces: Love—not merely as romance, but as *THE WILL TO LOVE*, as the driving force of life itself.

The Will to Love – Our Highest Calling

I believe what I am about to say might be a completely new concept— or at least one that has been forgotten. It is about the will to love. There are certain things that life seeks to teach us—not because we possess them in abundance, but because we are profoundly deprived of them. Things like love and truth. Love is something that must be learned.

One thing I know for certain: Love does not dwell within me. Perhaps within me dwells the longing to love someone truly or to be loved in return. But what about becoming love? What about learning to love?

When love enters the scene, nothing else matters. Education is irrelevant. Knowledge is irrelevant. Power is irrelevant. What truly matters is only love. Love is the driving force that helps us keep going.

It is the power that makes us believe in hope. We move, we exist, in love.

We suffer because love exists. We seek power because love is absent. Everything people do ultimately points to this: We are searching for love. And the painful truth is: Most people carry no truly loving heart within them. But the good news is: Love can be learned. And more than that—we must learn it. It is not just our responsibility to learn love—it is our obligation to become love, despite all the tragedies of life.

Think of all the unpleasant experiences we endure in life—when we are mocked or made to feel worthless. The moment we become aware of this, it begins to hurt. But can we still love the one who has brought us this hellish experience? Most of the time, we cannot. And if we can— perhaps that is exactly where we must change. When we seek revenge—do we not become the very hell we encountered? So, what is the better alternative? To become hell through pain—or to become the righteous sun through pain?

Man is planted on this Earth to learn to love the other. We must learn to love—in the way we are inwardly compelled to. The restlessness in our hearts, the pain in our minds—this is nothing but a thirst for unwavering devotion. The meaning of life is not to become a powerful person, not to create a meaningful life, not to influence others with words or abilities—but to learn. And what to learn? Love.

I remember a moment when I marveled at the wisdom of my father. No matter what happens—no matter what painful events occur—he says: "There is a higher good that lies beyond pain." And what is this higher good? It is love. One day, we will all learn to love—in a way that overcomes all obstacles. And then we will shine brighter than a thousand suns. The purpose of our lives is this: The will to love. It's that simple. We all know this. But are we willing to make this our will?

Truths are either simple or painful. And so a question arises: If the highest purpose of human existence is to learn to love—how can a person grow in love so that, despite all tragedies, they can remain in love? There is a widespread misconception that most things depend on our attitude or our thoughts, as if one could simply choose to learn to love out of free will. But precisely for this reason, I believe we need grace: Because we are not capable of doing the good we desire—but instead, we repeatedly do the evil we despise. This shows our true condition: How wretched we are. How fragile. How pitiful.

If we truly want to love—if we want to become love, which is our deepest reason for being—then we must ask for that grace that preserves us in love. The mere will is not enough. It has never been enough. In simple terms: Prayer is necessary for love to grow within us.

Scripture says it clearly: Ask, and it will be given to you (Matthew 7:7–8). But what should we ask for? Perhaps precisely what endures forever. Love does not fade. And if it does not fade, then it is worth asking for.

I used to ask myself:

Why pray at all?

What is the meaning of prayer in life?

Then I asked myself these questions: Do I love my neighbor? Can I forgive?

The answer was clear: No.

Then I knew—I needed prayer. For it is only through prayer that we, the wretched souls, continue to live under grace.

The Triangle of Truth

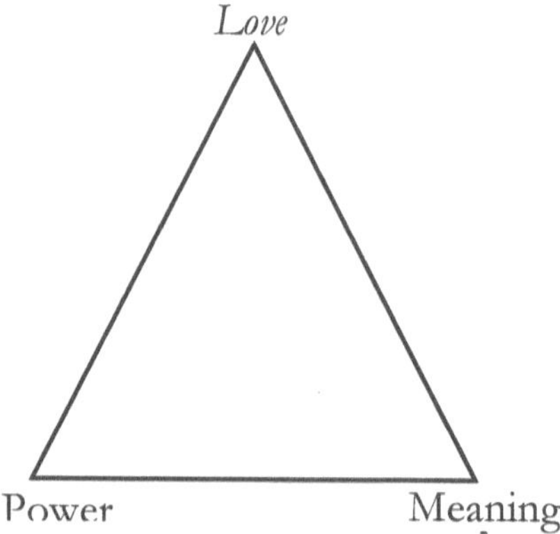

Here I have presented the Triangle of Truth – an image that describes the essence of existence, the reasons we believe, and the forces that compel us to live. As I have already said, each of these reasons has its own meaning in a person's life. But love – love remains at the top of this triangle. There are many ways to reach the highest. Some wretched souls recognize the truth only in the evening of their lives. Others, even more wretched, live as if the truth doesn't exist at all. Yet all our problems – our suffering, our confusion, our hatred – ultimately stem from a single deficiency: the lack of love.

Love is the essence of our soul. It heals. It grows. It blooms. The Scripture says: "Whoever loves has fulfilled the law" (Romans 13:810). Everything is now under the rule of love. For God himself reveals himself through love.

And yet, I know many people – especially married ones – who only pretend to have love. They play it like a role in a theater, but deep inside, they know it is empty. They remain trapped in their marriage – not because of the other, but because of themselves. They refuse to see the truth. They refuse to change. They reject inner growth. Their unwillingness to face the truth becomes their greatest obstacle.

I remember a quote from Friedrich Nietzsche. He said, "If you want to marry someone, ask yourself if you can imagine having a loving conversation with this person when you're old. If yes – then marry." He recognized what so many forget: the true meaning of love in marriage. Beauty fades. Power changes. Health ends. But love remains. The Triangle of Truth is not founded exclusively on love – but it must regard love as the most precious thing a person can strive for. Powerful people may advance, but that does not mean they will show us the right way. One thing I have noticed: the more powerful someone becomes, the more vulnerable they seem – for who truly knows what governs the hearts of powerful men and women? Perhaps it is the spirit of arrogance, or the spirit of conflict and deception. Pain is necessary to keep the heart of the inner warrior alive. Through pain, we become stronger, more fearless.

But beware – the mere search for meaning can turn into fanaticism. Then we forget everything else. Perhaps we even forget our wretched selves. But above all stands the spirit of love – the spirit that transforms all hatred into wisdom. The spirit that reminds us how broken we are. The spirit that shows us how much we depend on grace. The spirit that warns us to be vigilant when we fight against monsters.

I say this to all those wretched souls who feel pain – those who carry this nameless sorrow deep within them – just as I do. People will hurt us. They will laugh at us. Sometimes they will think of us as a joke. But remember this: we, the wretched, are the light of the world. We, the wretched, are the shining stars that the world ignores. We cry. We cry again. We cry desperately. But hear me: I, a wretched soul, want to tell you: we will rise. We will rise in glory. For it is written: "Blessed are those who mourn, for they will be comforted."

5

The Fate of the Wretched Soul

"Life and death I have set before you, now choose life, that you and your children may live." (Deuteronomy 30:19-20) Fate is given; it is not cultivated. Fate can never be created, but it creates us. I write all this for the wretched souls. And when I say "wretched souls," whom do I mean? I mean all of humanity, for every person is wretched in some way. We live a wretched life, not a fighting one. Our plans fail, we are knocked down, and we are born into pain. Every person who has created something new and beautiful has been accompanied by the delicate breath of pain. Without pain, beauty cannot exist. One should view misery and pain as a blessing, for when they are given, the magic begins—a magic that no soulmate can create. The wretched souls I encounter in everyday life lead exceptionally dull and unsatisfied lives. They say, "Why me?" But that is not a good question. What they should ask instead is: "Why not me?"

Why am I not growing stronger? Why is there no fire in me? When the right question is asked, the right answer also emerges. Perhaps we lose because we lack pain. Most people say that we create our own fate, that we are the masters of our own destiny. I do not believe in such fanaticism. I believe, rather, that the reaction to pain can be determined or developed—but not fate. Things happen that we never wished for. They do not consider our desires, and they do not show us what we will become. Every day, after morning comes evening, and most rest in the evening and sleep at night. Similarly, when chaos comes, we must remain in the chaos—not flee toward the morning. If we hurry to reach the morning, we must work harder and more desperately, completely exhausted and in a bad mood.

Let us view life this way: If we see everything through the eyes of an artist, then everything becomes beautiful—even darkness, chaos, order, and misery. People think that if they are born poor, they are destined to be losers, destined to become drinkers and wretched. But the truth is: We lose nothing in life. Life gives—it takes nothing back. What is given is given. Let us not believe that life is about losing. Life is about becoming.

In this chapter, I will tell how I—a wretched soul—realized that the richness of life does not lie in losing, but in becoming.

When the nights of our lives arrive, suddenly there is a fear of every aspect of life. It might be a whisper of hopelessness, which we are certain will consume us. I have experienced such things. I was devastatingly in pain and hopeless. Despite my pain, I longed for many things. I just wanted a word of hope, a tender touch, or a warm embrace. I pretended as if nothing was wrong with me, but everything was killing me inside. After returning from Germany, some showed me grace and gave me my position as a German teacher back. To be honest, I never wanted to be a German teacher at that time. I was incapable of teaching. I remember that whenever I turned to the board to write grammar, I did not see the board, but my heart—just as empty and full of pain as the board. No hope, no love, no expectations. I just wanted to tell someone that I was in pain, that I was a wretched man and needed help, but I found no one to share my pain with. I drowned in it, experienced it alone.

Now, you may ask if I had friends with whom I could share my thoughts. I had many friends. Many of them were alcoholics, and because I liked to drink, I connected with such people. They loved me when we drank together, but in sober times, I was not sure if they really liked me, and I didn't care about them either. We were friends with a glass in hand. There were also other friends—true friends— but I didn't call them and shared nothing with them because I never wanted to lie before them. I knew that once I started with one thing, I would have to tell them everything. So I didn't. On the other hand, some friends began calling me because I had not called them for weeks, but I ignored their calls and didn't call them back. They all felt that I had become arrogant, that I was avoiding them for this reason, but that was not the truth. I was more wretched than they were, the most wretched person among my friends. I no longer saw any light in my life. I began drinking and smoking heavily. I was far away from home, and people began to see me as a lost man—a drunkard at the age of 23. My mother, who knew I drank heavily, sometimes called me—not to offer words of hope but to criticize me. My father never called me. He neither supported me nor criticized me. There was no problem with my parents—they also had a difficult life. They had six children, and I was the oldest, so they had to take care of the others as well. I knew this and never said a word against them. Still, I decided to drink the cup of vinegar that God had given me.

I remember that in the times when I was deeply desperate, I went to the bar as quickly as possible after work, hoping that the drink I consumed would help me survive those painful hours. This is how my days passed… I bled every second. Sometimes it felt as if I was the pain, a person who had become it. What I sought in those days was a gentle touch and an encouraging word, and that was exactly what I lacked the most. I know there are people like me, perhaps even more wretched than I, who drown in blood and walk through the abyss. Let us continue our journey through the abyss, let us walk with our backs straight… Without fear, without despair. We, who walk through the abyss, are not alone. We are accompanied by many other wretched souls. We will all be strong; we do not just walk through the abyss, we stare it in the face. We, the wretched!

Hope and Despair

In the film The Shawshank Redemption, Red says, "Hope is a dangerous thing – it can drive a man insane." A philosophical insight that was already expressed by Friedrich Nietzsche: "Hope is in truth the worst of all evils, because it prolongs the torment of man."

In contrast, Andy in the film says, "Hope is a good thing, maybe the best of things. And no good thing ever dies." Hope is considered the core of our existence, for most people live with hope, without even knowing what they are truly hoping for. Most believe that someday everything will be okay – as if the chaos will end, and only order will remain. In a wretched world, the wretched souls long for a carefree, prosperous life. Perhaps this is the most hated and most often heard phrase in a person's life: "Everything will be fine." But what do they mean when they say everything will be fine?

They do not offer words of hope, but distort the truth so that one suffers again. Hope does not dwell in the fleeting, but in the eternal. Hope is everlasting.

Here's how I see it: Hope is the will to love. Life is wretched. It is a chain of tragedies. It is, in truth, painful. Yet we hope for a utopian life that does not exist. The element of hope resides in love, for love is the only viable answer to the problems of our existence. Hope and faith are intertwined. We believe that good things will happen – and that is good, it should be so. But what if our life is destined to end like that of the wretched souls in Auschwitz? Will we then fill our hearts with hate and malice – or, despite all tragedies, will we love our fate voluntarily, and even love our enemies? The will to love is not something simple. It must be actively sought – especially in times of chaos.

If love dwells within us, then there is truly hope – not hope for prosperity, but for contentment. Life today is very simple – but a hundred years ago, it was not like this. I have often thought about the lives of earlier philosophers, and I am amazed by the harshness of their lives. What made them philosophers was not their intellect, but their pain. Their unrequited love. They did not write words – they bled. Many things were written with blood, not just ink and quill. What made me a philosopher? It wasn't a degree. It wasn't a group of teachers. It wasn't the great philosophers I admire. It was pain. The pain I endured. I was forged in the university of pain. And now I live – not as a student, not as a German teacher, but as a philosopher. The rise of a modern philosopher – through pain and suffering. And in all of it, I found the will to love.

When we are hopeless, only despair remains in our hearts – and despair gives birth to hate, resentment, and weakness. If we do not direct our hearts toward the will to love, we will inevitably dwell in the will to revenge. These are the two true forces of will that drive humanity. Most people are obsessed with revenge. We believe power lies in striking back – inflicting upon others the same wounds they once inflicted upon us. But how true is this thought? Can good ever arise from the repetition of the same evil that once broke us? It is the spirit of resentment that ignites the will for revenge. In the modern world, revenge is often celebrated as strength, as the highest form of lived power. Yet this is the blindness of the heart — the inability to recognize that true strength lies not in retaliation, but in transcendence. In my darkest days, I too dreamed of paying everything back. I wanted to tear the world apart. And I knew — I knew — that I could do evil. But over time I realized: Even if painful experiences consume me, I must try to suffer silently — without resentment, without fear, without deceit, without revenge.

I am well aware of how overwhelming such an attitude seems. It appears impossible. Yet even if we — the wretched souls — fail at these highest and noblest ideals, we must not call that failure. We will. We transcend ourselves precisely through the better failure. And thus, we become what we are meant to be. The will for revenge is the highest form of evil. It takes everything from us — even our own life. We are not called to take revenge, but to forget and forgive.

If we seek freedom — freedom from resentment, deceit, and envy — life becomes like poetry: elegant, painful, and beautiful. The wise must make their life beautiful. Some are born with beauty, but others make life beautiful. We, the modern philosophers — the modern wise ones — are obligated to make our life beautiful. And when the time has passed, and death has devoured us, then people should say about us:

"They were the wretched souls — but in their time, they made everything beautiful."

Existential Invisibility

Most people long to be seen – as they truly are, with all their inner potential. Yet the sad truth of our existence is this: no one will ever truly understand us. People fear being misunderstood more than they fear not being understood at all. There were times in my life when I felt the abyssal curse of existence—not because I was lonely, not because I suffered, not because I lacked money—but because I never found a person who truly understood me. Such a person never existed, and perhaps, they never will.

Existential invisibility reveals to us, in a brutal way, the misery of human existence. Imagine this: an angel takes us to the deepest depths of the hearts of all those we have ever encountered, and shows us that we are distorted, wrong, and incomplete in their eyes. That they have never seen us as we truly are. And that they never will—no matter how much power, money, or intelligence we possess.

Could we bear this truth? Without fear? Without judgment? Would we be able to laugh in the face of the abyss—to dance on its face— although no one recognizes us? Not the living. Not even the dead?

I have been fighting this demon for years. It hurts to know that we are alone on this journey, that we are misunderstood. No philosopher in history has ever been fully understood. They wrote the truth—and the world distorted it. Existential invisibility destroys marriages, alienates children from their parents, drives great souls into the abyss. The greatest men in history were misunderstood. And then they were killed. But greatness does not die—it is reborn posthumously. All of this makes me sad. But I keep going. I dance on the face of the abyss. And I will rise—like the morning star. Even Jesus was misunderstood by his mother and brothers in the New Testament. No wonder they killed him. This is the fate of all wretched souls.

So why should we fear invisibility? Fear breeds weakness. And weak people die weak. The healing lies in acceptance—in moving forward without looking back. Even if existence is blind—one sees: you. And I. We can look into our own soul, and when we look inward, we rise. We confront the absurd. And we keep going—free.

When we truly love a person, we do not only see them as they are, but as they can become. Through love, one overcomes existential invisibility. What deeply frightens me is this: the more I try to understand others, the deeper I look into their souls, the clearer I see an emptiness within them—a void, filled with darkness, that prevents them from seeing what they should see. Love is the remedy here. It does not merely build beliefs; it acknowledges all shortcomings—and goes beyond good and evil.

It is often said that no one will ever love us the way we desire. If this assumption is true, it follows that no one will ever truly see us as we are—unless true love resides in their hearts. As wretched as we may be, we are not defined by our suffering alone, but by love. It is love that teaches us to suffer silently, to accept our wretched selves, and to face the dragon that will burn us to our core.

Be Watchful – *γρηγορέω*

In Matthew 26:41, Jesus says: "Watch and pray, so that you will not fall into temptation." The Greek word for "watch" is *γρηγορέω* – it means to stay awake, to be vigilant. Again and again, Christ calls His disciples to remain watchful. Not just physically, but especially spiritually. But why be watchful? Why should we, wretched people, even stay awake? Because we know that the apocalypse is coming. We know the monsters are real. Whether what seeks to devour us is death or life, we don't know. But we roll up our sleeves like warriors, and we smile in the face of the roaring beasts that want to tear our souls apart. We don't crawl. We don't sneak. We stand tall – like warriors. Our fate may be suffering. But falling is not our end. We rise again – and we must rise again. Never ask "How?" – the "How" brings confusion. It shatters trust. It is better to find a "Why." Because the "Why" ignites our inner fire. Vigilance is power. It is the seed of authority. The root of influence. In the modern world, most people lack this: vigilance. They have built huts – in their phones. They forget to lift their gaze. They forget to straighten their backs. And how can one go forward if one does not look ahead? Those who do not look ahead, stumble. And those who stumble, fall. But we were not planted to fall. We were planted to grow.

One reason I stopped drinking alcohol is that it does not elevate our consciousness – it diminishes it. It does not help us stay awake – it numbs us. But to be honest: I haven't fully stopped. I drink occasionally. Because I still believe in the Dionysian spirit of chaos. But even in chaos, one must remain vigilant. Even in madness, the warrior needs watchful eyes. Wretched people must stay awake. Because vigilance is a power that God has given us. Not all evils can be defeated by physical strength. Some only bow to the watchful gaze. Most people suffer foolishly – because they weren't watchful. Because they didn't see what they should have seen. Because they didn't hear what they should have heard. Though we are wretched – we are vigilant. And because we are vigilant, we are dangerous.

"Vigilance is the path to immortality; Inattention is the path to death. The wise, who are vigilant, do not die; The fools, who are inattentive, are already like dead."

— The Dhammapada, translated by Juan Mascaró
This quote is attributed to Juan Mascaró, a Spanish writer and translator. He says that vigilance is not a weakness; it is the path to immortality. And that is precisely what I emphasize here – I, a wretched man, am indeed wretched, but not weak. Indeed wretched, but not dead. Indeed wretched, but I love the wretchedness. Our fate is this: to be vigilant, to be awake—not entangled in trivial things, but transforming every pain and every suffering into something beautiful. Perhaps through art, through writing, through love. We must recognize the inner "We." There is existential invisibility, there is hope and despair. No matter— we can always be vigilant. I once thought that what was to come was destruction and chaos, but I was wrong. In the end, what awaits us is not the apocalypse, but courage—the courage that will lead us through the fiercest storm. If God is almighty, He calls us to be mighty men—not men who slumber in comfort, waiting for life to pass them by.

6

The Philosophy of Obligation

Responsibility and Obligation

Responsibility and obligation are two fundamentally different concepts – and it's worth understanding their true difference. Most people only talk about responsibility. Hardly anyone thinks about obligation. In this chapter, I want to show you: We are obligated to certain things. And by the end of this chapter, you'll understand why. Society teaches us to become more responsible as we grow older. But I have often asked myself: Should we fulfill our responsibilities because we are obligated? Who has given us this responsibility in the first place? And why should we even fulfill it? I believe: Responsibility is not granted. It is chosen. Imagine a man who decides to marry. He takes on the responsibility of caring for his wife and children. This burden – perhaps the greatest joy and also the deepest sorrow – he has placed upon himself. No one forced him to do so. He chose it voluntarily. Responsibility can be passed on. If we fail to fulfill our responsibility, someone else can take it on. But obligation goes deeper. Obligation is non-transferable.

Many people never ask themselves the question: What am I truly obligated to in life? And even if you ask them – who could give a clear answer? I have struggled with this question for a long time. And today, I believe I have found the answer: Our highest obligation is to live. To keep living. No death before we die. We lack many answers, but questions are never in short supply. Who should we ask? Who

tells us the harsh truth of life? Who gives us comfort? Some say: God. I don't know if God is the answer to all this misery. But I believe: Our God is a silent God. A God who prefers silence over words. A God who loves the wretched more than the perfect. We have a thousand reasons to want to die. But perhaps only one reason to live: Because we are obligated to do so. Not because we hope for a better tomorrow. Not because the best days are yet to come. Who knows what comes next? Angels or demons? Let them come. We will continue to live. Not because it is our responsibility – but because it is our obligation. And because there is no escape. We must live until we die. No death before we die.

In the myth of Sisyphus, Camus ends with the sentence that we must imagine Sisyphus as happy. But he never says that Sisyphus was really happy as he rolled the boulder up the hill again and again. Life is absurd – but to escape nihilism, Camus says, we can imagine Sisyphus as happy. But for me, there is no truth in this myth.

I have often asked myself: Why should we consider him happy? What is the truth here? Was he really happy doing this over and over again? Probably not. It is impossible to truly be happy with the most absurd things in life. Let's assume this myth is our fate. Then we will do what Sisyphus did – not because it brings us joy, but because we are obligated to do it. We are obligated to do the most absurd things in life.

That's why I say: One should not imagine Sisyphus as happy. Because he was not. The best thing is to recognize that sometimes life becomes so absurd that we must choose the hard path – and still continue living. The philosophy of obligation reminds us: We are born to certain obligations, and we must fulfill them – no matter how difficult it is to roll that boulder.

The Weight of Responsibility

It is impossible to live without responsibility. Each of us is called to carry a burden. In Greek mythology, we find many figures who embodied this responsibility as if it were their tragic fate – one of them was Prometheus. He recognized the fragility of humankind and made the decision to love them – as one of them. It was a decision that, once made, could never be undone. And he knew exactly how hard this path would be. Yet, he never looked back. He acted like a tragic hero. Responsibility does not mean a comfortable life. What makes life adventurous is precisely responsibility.

When we voluntarily take on our burden and move forward, we become like Prometheus – the tragic hero who loved pain, who thought differently. Responsibility is a burden – yet it is a burden we must carry. Not because we are destined for destruction, but because we are called into the unknown. And by facing the unknown, we become stronger. If responsibility is a burden, then obligation cannot be seen as one. Because there is only one thing to which we are truly obligated: to keep living. We are obligated to live – and to live without resentment against life itself. Think of the tragic heroes: Jesus, Prometheus, Frankl, Éponine from Les Misérables. Life hurled pure chaos at them. But how they responded – that was the amazing part. Life cursed them. And they blessed life. This is the kind of life we are called to live. A life that seeks no meaning. It doesn't ask why. It knows: life itself is worth

living. We must see our life as an obligation. And when life screams and rages against us – and yet we bless our existence – that is a spiritual act of worship. Not figuratively speaking – no, it is worship.

All worldly blessings are a curse when they meet arrogance. But suffering – when carried with love and without resentment – is holy.

I have already spoken about the primary obligation of our lives – it is simple but profound: to live. But beyond that, I also believe in certain responsibilities and tasks that we are meant to fulfill. Why? Because people hunger for meaning. They long for testimonies. They love stories, watch movies, seek adventures – and want to create something that lasts. I often think of Dostoevsky. His novels have helped countless souls recognize difficult truths. But imagine – what if he hadn't written them? If he had not fulfilled his task? The world would have been darker. Many wretched souls would have quietly died, without even a spark of hope.

I know this silence. In my darkest hours, I survived only because of one sentence – a sentence from Nietzsche: "What doesn't kill me makes me stronger." I knew these experiences would not kill me. And if they didn't kill me, what would they do? They would make me stronger. I believed his words. I carried my pain in silence. His words were a light before me in the darkness. And then I wonder: if Nietzsche hadn't written those words – what would have become of me? Maybe I would have broken down like a weak man. Who knows? But I did not. I held on. I became stronger. Nietzsche – who was hardly noticed in his time – was reborn after his death. Today, he lives on through his words. And there lies his victory: he did what he was obligated to do.

Regarde profondément – Look Deeply

The phrase *regarde profondément* comes from French and means: "Look deeply." It's not merely a call to see but a summons to recognize the deepest truths. In the previous chapter, I spoke of existential invisibility – that agonizing feeling of being truly unseen by anyone. Here, I offer an answer to that: we must look deeply. What distinguishes us humans is the depth of our gaze – our ability to see without prejudice, to look beyond the surface, to recognize what is hidden, and to break through the facades behind which people conceal themselves. What I have come to understand in life is this: people want to be seen. Not just physically – but emotionally and spiritually. Yet we humans are masters of hiding. We rarely show who we truly are. Many do not feel worthless because they do not know their value, but because the people around them have never recognized it.

Think of the life of Fyodor Dostoevsky. He loved a woman named Anna Grigorievna. She first came into his life as his stenographer. Despite her young age, she saw something eternal in him. Others may have seen Dostoevsky only as the gambler, the sick man, the addict. But Anna looked deeper. She saw not only who he was – she saw who he could become in ten years. We do not need a thousand people to look deeply. We need the one – the true one – who looks into us. People die inwardly, not because they lack strength, but because no one recognizes the gold in their soul.

There are those who desperately seek to show themselves, who put on a moral display, performing good deeds for the sake of appearance – but this only brings emptiness. It is a path into chaos, not into love. The wretched, however, are humble enough to admit their brokenness.

And in them, I always see a light – a weak but real light that can guide us through the darkness. I believe: misery is a blessing. And perhaps

– just perhaps – one day we will meet someone who looks into our wretched soul. And in that gaze, our torment transforms into an eternal elixir of life.

If I may express this in biblical terms, I remember the Gospel of John, chapter 1, verses 47-48. Jesus says to Nathanael: "Behold, an Israelite indeed, in whom is no deceit!" And then he continues: "I saw you." These three words – "I saw you" – deeply touch me. To truly see someone – how beautiful is that? And how blessed is the one who is seen? For me, Jesus is the perfect example of a true human being. He sees the invisible. And when we learn to see the humble and the wounded, we ignite a light in them – a light that may one day lead thousands to hope.

7

A Letter to the Wretched Souls

Why I wrote this wretched book for the wretched people

Let me tell you why I decided to write this wretched book for the wretched people. One day, I was reading the Bible, and suddenly I came across a verse that struck me deeply. It comes from Paul:

"O wretched man that I am! Who shall deliver me from the body of this death?" (Romans 7:24).

He said: "O wretched man that I am!" – such a powerful verse. He acknowledged his own wretchedness, something most people never do. After deeply reflecting on this verse, I suddenly felt the urge to write a book on this theme: "Ich elender Mensch."

I had always wanted to write, and originally, I had planned a different book.

But a voice – perhaps my own voice of conscience – said to me: Not that book. Begin first with the misery of life.

And so I was convinced: I must write this book. When I began planning, I didn't yet know exactly what I would write – but I had an idea: I must write a letter to the wretched.

And this letter I am writing is for all wretched people. I didn't write this book just because I felt like it, but because there was a deep, divine inspiration behind this work.

Perhaps God is making me an instrument to speak to the wretched – to those who are seen as failures, who have failed in life, who live without hope.

We, the wretched – we are unloved, but we are lovable.

We, the wretched – we live in darkness, but we are the light of this world.

Letter to the Alcoholics

People who drink are perhaps the most misunderstood souls of all time. Society often treats drinking as an absolute form of evil. Maybe that's because many of the world's worst deeds were committed under the influence of alcohol. Yes – alcohol kills. It gives no life. It is poison, it is madness, it is bullshit.

But what about the people who drink it – are they evil? Are they worthless? Are they the curse of this world? I don't believe that.

Humans are meant to drink water. But those whose lives have hardened into stone sometimes drink alcohol instead of water. Not out of joy – but to survive.

Alcoholics are not demons. They are people who drink liquor like water because their souls are parched, and the world has forgotten to rain on them.

People always shout that drugs must be eradicated. And although alcohol is often seen as hedonistic, it's sometimes not pleasure – but despair.

I remember a time in my life when loneliness had such a firm grip on me that I had no one to speak a single word to.

One evening, I noticed a group of young men who lived near my apartment. Out of a longing for connection, I asked them if they wanted to drink something. They said yes – hesitantly, because they had little money. I told them: "It's not about the money. I'll pay. No matter what it costs."

But what my soul was begging for was never alcohol. I was begging for closeness. For someone who would talk to me. Who would offer me a word of encouragement. A gentle voice. A hand on my shoulder. Something human – just so I could breathe for a few minutes.

That's how my days were after I got kicked out of Germany.

Today, when I think back on that time, I know: I didn't want the bottle. I wanted love – that kind of love that teaches you how to breathe again when silence crushes your chest.

But the young men I drank with didn't see me. They drank with me, but they didn't look deep enough. And I was still alone.

It's pointless to preach to people that they should stop drinking or smoking. They know exactly that it's killing them.

What they need isn't a moral lecture – they need someone who sees them. Truly sees them. Who recognizes what they're searching for in smoke and in the bottle.

If you give them love – the elixir of life – then I swear to you:

The person who smokes ten cigarettes a day might smoke only eight
that day.

Letter to the Broken Ones

There are people who are crushed under the weight of existence—

and yet, they carry their pain and still breathe.

It is not a good idea to count our miseries.

A better act would be to silently enjoy the beauty of nature.

We long for love, we long for a beautiful future, but

nothing will come to us; what comes is pain and misery…

and it often comes in our worst moments.

I will never tell you that a time will come when everything will be fine!

No. I can't say that—because I don't believe it.

But I do believe in the present moment, in our breath right now.

That is all we have.

A friend recently told me that the only thing that burns for him
is a cigarette— and he is literally dying for that burn and that
smoke.
This isn't just true for his life; it's true for mine as well.

We are broken people.
Let's acknowledge that.
But we are never shattered. We are in pain— but we
have not given up.

I remember a moment when a friend told me that his refuge isn't
God or any deity—
it's travel.
It's the only time he can relax.
He cannot relax at home or with people he knows.

I know many young men are struggling with similar battles.
But it doesn't matter.
Let us not dwell on it.

Let us look at the sea and recognize how calm and full of
love it is.

Like Meursault said: It means nothing—nothing means anything.
It doesn't matter what happens. Those who live entirely for love
will always say: It doesn't matter. And in that— there is a strange
kind of peace.

Letter to the Betrayed

The pain of betrayal burns hotter than the blaze of a thousand suns. I
have been betrayed – more than once. And every time, I burned.

Betrayed by people I trusted. People I believed had valued my
closeness.

I remember exactly what happened a year ago – my time in Germany.
My first journey abroad. I had worked hard. Learned German with
dedication and patience. And most of all: I carried hope within me.

I was convinced: I will fly to Germany and live a happy life.

But everything fell apart.

My life shattered before my eyes. Every carefully crafted plan was
destroyed. Some of my classmates made accusations against me. Part
of it was true. But the most serious ones – I hadn't done them.

Then came the verdict from my boss:

"You must leave Germany today."

In that moment, I stood at the edge of the abyss.

I knew: If I return, no light will ever touch my life again.

I begged for two more days. Two days to maybe save the visa, to keep the dream alive.

In vain. My boss accompanied me all the way to the airport.

Just before goodbye, he hugged me. And I cried. Not just because of the dismissal.

I cried because that hug was more than a gesture. In the midst of unbearable pain, I suddenly felt love – something words cannot capture.

Before I left, he even gave me some money.

Friends had turned against me. But I carry no hatred. No bitterness. No desire for revenge.

My fate – wounded, burned, broken – I accept it.

No matter how hard it gets – I go on.

What awaits all of us is death.

But that day, my transformation began.

That day, I became the prophet of the wretched.

I know the taste of betrayal.

I have experienced isolation.

I was addicted to alcohol.

I was afraid of my own existence.

Afraid even to breathe.

And that's why I speak to you, my wretched brothers and sisters:

Life gets harder – second by second.

And still, we go on.

We live by the philosophy of obligation.

They will burn us.

They will betray us.

They will cast us out.

But we, the wretched, walk on – toward the path of redemption.

And yes – we forgive.

Letter to the Unloved

It is a universal truth:

When we love someone with all the generosity of our heart, that

person may not love us back in the way we hope.

Everyone, at some point, will taste the pain of unrequited love.

I have known this sorrow in many forms.

When I was dismissed from Germany, it felt like the greatest pain I could bear was the loss of hope— the sense that life might no longer hold meaning.

But months later, as I began rebuilding my future, I discovered a light within me, longing for company— a companion who would stand by me, even in the darkest moments.

During my studies, I met a woman.
To the outside world, she was nothing remarkable.
But to me, she was everything.

I remember the moment I first saw her— thoughts raced through my mind:

Could I learn to love her?
Could I walk beside her until the end of my days?

But those were merely the desires of my heart.
In the end, it doesn't matter. I loved her, even though she never loved me in return.

My love for her is my testimony—

a sign of life itself.

Because if we can love, then we are alive.

The dead do not love.

The living do.

It doesn't matter whether love is returned or not. The question isn't

whether we are loved— but whether we are capable of loving. And if

we are, then that love is sacred— more healing than anything else.

If I were to tell Meursault, the hero in Camus' The Stranger, about

my unreturned love, he'd probably shrug and say,

"It doesn't matter. The sea is beautiful today."

And in a way, he's right— it doesn't matter.

But that doesn't mean we should become indifferent.

Love— even when rejected— is of immeasurable

value.

It is a testimony of our aliveness.

To the wretched souls, I say this:

Do not fear to love.

Through our pain, we must face the brokenness of our

hearts.

For it is through that brokenness that we find

what truly keeps us alive— our ability to love,

regardless of the outcome.

Letter to the Isolated

I write this letter to all who are isolated.

Isolation is an unbearable pain. Those who have felt it know: this life
has not been kind.

Part of why I love Nietzsche, Kafka, Jesus, Dostoevsky, and Frankl
lies in this very truth— they were all isolated.

They were precious—hidden sapphires—and yet, unrecognized.

This is what I call existential invisibility:

You are worthy, but no one sees you.   You

are an undiscovered jewel. And you, who

suffer like I do— we are

holy.

Let me tell you a truth in the form of a picture.

People often say,

"There is a light in every person." A light meant

to shine in the darkness.

But I say to you:

Our heart is full of light.

And that light is covered by the surface of the heart.

When pain, sorrow, and unbearable experiences enter our heart, they

tear cracks into it. And the more we suffer, the more cracks emerge—

maybe a hundred, maybe a hundred thousand.

And we must go on living with those cracks.

It hurts.

On some days, it is almost unbearable.

And then we weep.

And we ask:

Why, God? Why do You allow this?

What could possibly come from all this suffering?

Are we cursed—or are we chosen?

Perhaps—just perhaps—   the cracks are

not a curse, but preparation.

Because when the heart breaks open completely, the hidden light

begins to shine.

It spreads into the world. And this light—this divine fire—

can change everything.

If we accept the pain—truly accept it—without bitterness, something

wondrous happens.

The cracks become paths of transformation.

Do not fear your cracks, dear soul.

They are preparing you for a miracle you would hardly believe.

Let me speak plainly:

I, too, am isolated.

Since youth, I've walked alone.

It is a heavy burden.

Sometimes, I cry aloud from the weight.

I know that I am worthy.

And yet, no one sees me.

And that—more than anything—hurts.

But you— you who are isolated— you are not

alone.

Even if we are far from each other, we are sailing the same boat.

To my fellow sufferers…

To the drinkers…   To the unloved…

To the broken… To the invisible—

I say:

We are not saints. But we are sacred.

We are not lighthouses. But we are torches.

We suffer—and still we choose life.

And it is exactly there that our greatness lies.

We are in pain, and yet we learn—day by day—

to love.

Even those who do not love us back.

Even our enemies.

And maybe, one day, the light within us will shine so clearly that

others will finally see what God saw all along:

That we were never invisible.

We were only holy enough to remain hidden.

8

The Chackovian Principle –
The Philosophy of the Wretched Soul

"This is the Chackovian Principle: The wretched man is the redeemed man, if he accepts his wretchedness."

At first glance, the Chackovian Principle may sound provocative. But those who truly understand it will recognize a profound truth: when a wretched soul willingly embraces its wretchedness—without bitterness, with an open heart—it undergoes a transformation. Not outwardly, but inwardly. Not socially, but existentially.

Who are the wretched?

They are not merely the poor or the suffering in the conventional sense. No. They are those whom the world despises.

The Apostle Paul cries out in his Letter to the Romans (7:21):

"So I find this law at work: Although I want to do good, evil is right there with me."

He wrestles with himself. He wants to do good—and ends up doing evil.

He is torn. Broken. Wretched. And in his inner agony he cries:

"O wretched man that I am!"

This wretchedness is not merely psychological pain. It is a spiritual battle.

In today's world, however, wretchedness is understood differently. People are no longer considered wretched because they wrestle with sin or meaning, but because they have failed in life's external terms. These are the ones who wanted a good, happy life—but life broke them.

They have no prestigious career, no societal recognition.

They have fallen.

They have been betrayed.

They are unloved and misunderstood.

Some choose death—hoping to escape their misery.

But others—the stronger ones—choose life.

Not because they believe society will one day honor them or reward them with success. No.

They live because they have recognized their obligation.

They do not live out of hope, but out of loyalty.

They do not hate their fate—they love it.

Not passively, but without resentment—with a quiet amor fati.

These wretched ones—they are greater than the millionaire who lives off the applause of the world.

The wretched are the sinners, the failures, the broken, the misunderstood.

And I say to you:

You are the redeemed.

What Society Gets Wrong

In our society, a person's worth is measured by the size of their wallet.

This remains true, no matter how wicked someone may be—if one possesses wealth, all things bow before them.

There is power in becoming desirable, and society finds desirability in resources.

Money, the modern god, is now the highest proof of competence.

The wretched souls must never listen to what the world says—for the world is fluent in lies.

Humanity excels at twisting the truth to justify its desires.

One thing I have come to realize:

Society is a blind man led by a blind dictator.

It exiles the wretched—yet these very outcasts see with the clearest eyes.

The best thing one can do is choose a different, harder path.

Why?

Because the hard path reveals new horizons.

Pain cannot be avoided; danger is not to be feared.

There are roads we must walk barefoot—some paved with fire.

And yes, sometimes it is unbearable—but what is better? To avoid

the fire and remain weak, or to walk through it and become strong?

A happy, pleasure-filled life may belong to the ordinary.

But not to the Oversoul.

The Oversoul lives a life of suffering and adventure—for only
through suffering can we confront chaos and ascend to heaven.

Society teaches us to beg for love.

The wretched teach us to carry love like a double-edged sword.

This sword is forged in sorrow and guided by truth.

As I wrote about existential invisibility—it is pointless to want to be
seen by a world that prefers blindness.

This world mocks the truthful and rewards the wicked.

And so we accept our invisibility.

We move forward.

Silently. Defiantly. Until our last breath.

The end is our hope.

Beginnings are easy—but to reach the place we are truly destined for— that is the test.

Think of those who rose from the ashes: Nietzsche, Dostoevsky, Jesus, St. Dismas.

They were cursed, broken, betrayed, exiled.

The most wretched of men.

And yet—they live on.

Through their words, their actions, their creative spirits.

Redemption does not belong to the powerful or the rulers.

If they are already above—what is there to rise from?

Redemption is not success.

It is survival.

It belongs to the wretched, the lost, the failed, the sinners.

We, the wretched, are the true revolution.

Redemption is Survival

The redemption I speak of is not success.

It is survival.

The hardest thing in life is: to survive.

And it is exactly this that earns respect.

I write these words because I believe they will help me survive.

This is not a polished, flawless work.

It is the cry of a wretched soul who believes in redemption.

Let me tell you a story from the Gospel of John.

During the crucifixion of Jesus, there hung beside him a thief— now known as St. Dismas.

He was never a good man.

Never a successful man.

He was wretched.

The Romans crucified the wretched.

Perhaps the good thief knew who Jesus was, and yet he lived an unjust life.

And still, Jesus spoke to him:

"Today you will be with me in paradise."

The good thief survived.

He survived through his humility.

I believe in the power of humility—even though I often fail to be humble myself.

The unsuccessful, the broken, the misunderstood—they have nothing to be proud of.

They live in the abyss.

But even the abyss is covered with love.

Therefore, I say: Even the wretched can be saved.

Even they can be loved by God—if they accept their fate and live with humility.

What the modern world lacks is humility.

And why?

Because it has not been broken.

Not yet.

Look at the elderly.

They are forgiving.

They are loving.

They are divine.

Why?

Because they carry more pain than we can fathom.

Only pain strips us of our arrogance.

I was once a person who thought life was safe.

I had nothing to fear.

But slowly, I began to break.

I became an alcoholic. A smoker. A failure. A loser.

At 24, I didn't even have a degree.

People asked me:

"What the hell have you done for the last ten years?"

I had no answer.

But one thing I knew:

It hurt.

And this pain—it made me stronger.

A Personal Confession to All Those Who Suffer

I remind you—once again: We, who suffer, who are crushed by the weight of existence—we are not lost souls. We are redeemed.

And redemption does not mean prosperity.

Whoever is aware of their own wretchedness will live in humility, will accept their fate—and love it.

Most people fear death.

But I believe there is something even more terrifying: life.   For to live is no easy task.

Whoever reflects on existence, who seeks meaning, is often overwhelmed by their own consciousness.

If this book overwhelms you—if it feels incomplete—then remember one thing:

We humans do not understand love.

What we lack the most is love.

What we most need to learn is love.

I love a woman.

And I am still afraid to tell her.

I have loved many – quietly and secretly.

And I know: we all do this.

We love – and we hide it.

But what truly frightens me is not rejection, but that love makes me vulnerable.

And yet I long for it.

I am a man with a Nietzschean spirit – and a great desire for the will to love.

Love is the most beautiful thing there is – even toward our enemies.

It is what transforms them.

Even pain has its meaning: It brings us closer to love.

What men learn to love, women teach.

What women learn to love, men teach.

Modern voices say that one gender does not need the other to live –

and yes, that may be true.

But if you love without having learned to love – then that is death.

As Nietzsche said: the death of God.

I, a wretched man, have written this for the wretched – so that we

may learn love – and make our brief existence on this earth a little

more beautiful.

Afterword

We fight and dance

This book is the cry of a wretched soul.

As I wrote it, I made a quiet promise to myself:

I will only write what I believe to be true.

And that's exactly what I did.

This book is not written for everyone – especially not for those who do not see themselves as wretched.

If you are one of them, then I'm sorry: This is not your book.

But to my wretched friends – those who have tasted the night and still breathe – this is for you.

I am here, I fight. For you. For me.

I know my fate.

One day, a wretched person will rise.

He will read this book and whisper in his heart, "This man bled in words what I could not bleed."

And that is exactly why I wrote.

We fight and we dance on the edge of the abyss.

Acknowledgments

I thank you, Jesus – you are the most powerful person I have ever seen in history. Not because you prevented pain, but because you stayed with me in the suffering.

I thank my parents, who stood by my side in the darkest times of my life. Your love was the last light that never went out.

Especially, I thank my father – you are my hero.

I thank Alfred, my wretched friend. You are becoming, brother. Keep going.

I thank Justin, my brother and friend. We both know: What doesn't kill us makes us stronger.

I thank Dr. Vandhana, my psychology teacher, for not seeing me as I am, but as what I can become. Such eyes change lives.

About the Author

Joyal K Chacko is a philosopher, author, German teacher, and psychology student. He is 24 years old—unemployed, but not lost. His life is not a resume, but a rebellion: against nihilism, against invisibility, against the quiet despair of modern existence.

He writes for the wretched—for those who feel unseen, unloved, unnoticed.

Ich elender Mensch is not just a book; it is a mirror for the soul brave enough to look into it.

In his works, Joyal explores themes such as existential invisibility, the will to love, and the unshakable commitment to life. His influences range from Nietzsche to Kierkegaard, Viktor Frankl, and Christ. He walks, he thinks, he suffers—and he writes.

This is his first book. But it will not be his last.

"I have fallen, but I have not broken."